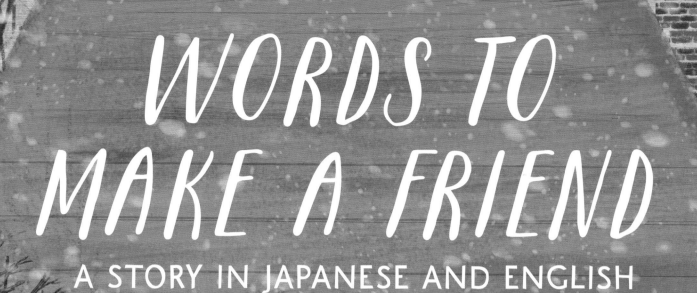

WORDS TO
MAKE A FRIEND

A STORY IN JAPANESE AND ENGLISH

by DONNA JO NAPOLI
pictures by NAOKO STOOP

RANDOM HOUSE STUDIO · NEW YORK

Push and mush.

Tataite tataite.

Giza giza.

Zig zag.

Shiver shiver.

Buru buru.

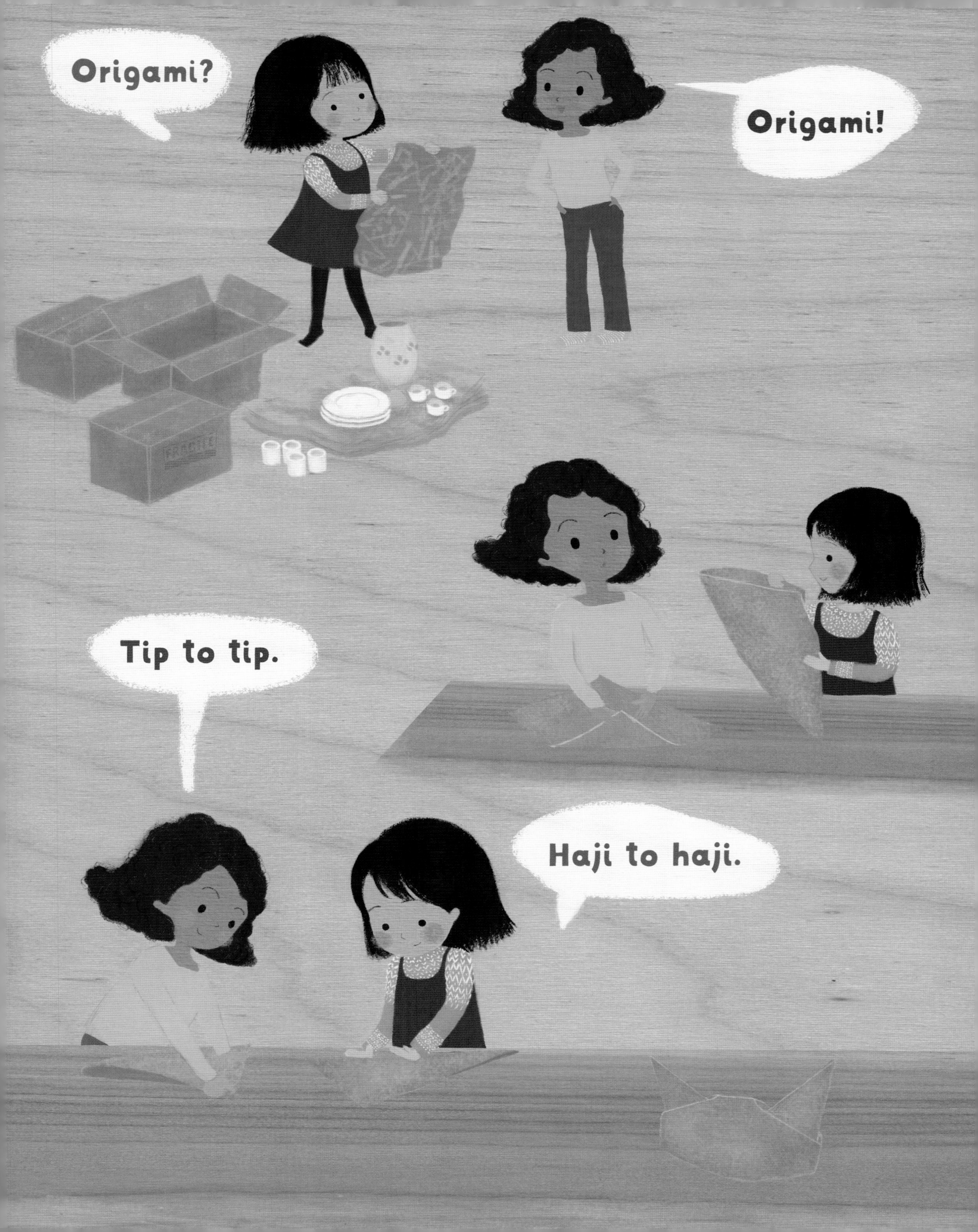
Origami?
Origami!
Tip to tip.
Haji to haji.

My grandparents came to the United States speaking Italian. One of them learned English and made friends with Americans easily, but three of them preferred not to use English and had only Italian friends. Maybe that's why I've always been fascinated by how people who speak different languages begin the journey toward friendship. How do people climb over the initial language barrier most words put up? The girls in this story do it with their actions, yes, but also by choosing to say words whose sounds and rhythms fit well with what they mean. They look at the bloopy snow monster they have built and say "botteri" and "roly poly," words with sounds that seem round and heavy themselves. The girls make a game out of saying such words, tossing them in the air almost like tossing a ball so that the other one can catch their meaning. Finally, they laugh together, and laughter is understood in any language. What better way to start a friendship?

To my many Japanese students over the years who have taught me about mimetics, and especially to Elizabeth Wiseman, who figured out how they work —D.J.N.

For my unlikely friends, Cheryl, Mark, and Casi —N.S.

ILLUSTRATOR'S NOTE

It is not easy to be both new and different. My story is in some ways very similar to the Japanese girl in the book. Although I was an adult when I first moved to Canada from Japan, I still see myself in her very much.

Making new friends in a new place can be challenging no matter who you are or what you look like, but having a language barrier makes that hurdle even more difficult to overcome. What I've learned, though, is that it doesn't matter how many words you know or how good your pronunciation or grammar is. Friendships start when we share something of ourselves with another person. I was shy as a girl and still am, but I have made some of my dearest friends not with sharing a lot of words but by sharing experiences. The two girls in this story became friends sharing a snowstorm and the fun of creating a snow monster. I've made friends painting, cooking, and dancing together.

Text copyright © 2021 by Donna Jo Napoli
Jacket art and interior illustrations copyright © 2021 by Naoko Stoop

All rights reserved. Published in the United States by Random House Studio, an imprint of Random House Children's Books, a division of Penguin Random House LLC, New York. • Random House Studio and the colophon are registered trademarks of Penguin Random House LLC. Visit us on the Web! rhcbooks.com • Educators and librarians, for a variety of teaching tools, visit us at RHTeachersLibrarians.com

Library of Congress Cataloging-in-Publication Data is available upon request.
ISBN 978-0-593-12227-3 (trade)
ISBN 978-0-593-12228-0 (lib. bdg.)
ISBN 978-0-593-12229-7 (ebook)

The illustrations were rendered in mixed media on plywood and finished digitally.

The text of this book is set in Mrs. Lollipop Fill in varying sizes.

Interior design by Rachael Cole

MANUFACTURED IN CHINA
10 9 8 7 6 5 4 3 2 1
First Edition

The Aquinnah Public Library
1 Church Street
Aquinnah, MA 02535